Papa—Can You Hear Me?

Short Stories by Samuel I. Lora

PublishAmerica
Baltimore

ISBN: 978-1-60749-321-1
PUBLISHED BY PUBLISHAMERICA, LLLP
www.publishamerica.com
Baltimore

Printed in the United States of America

Obviously, my father had a lot to do with inspiring this piece, but I
want to appreciate the following individuals:
A mother and a sister that have constantly been there.
This book doesn't need to be named accordingly, as the whole equals
the sum of its parts.
A life that has been shared completely and selflessly between four
soul-mates.

Monica
Sebas ◇ Tulia
Samuel

To Monica & Tulia
The great gifts life has let me have
Besos/Abrazos
Samuel

To the child and the wondrous stories of such reality: NOT imagination.

Bitter

Graffiti Blues

"Eat your dinner!" the father exclaimed toward the boy. The boy sat cross-armed and resentfully grabbed a hold of his metal weapon, letting the fork do the feeding. He swallowed as his eyes, slightly hidden behind his crouching eyebrows, perforated holes of hate on his father's body. He wasn't pleased with the dismissal of his worries. Tomorrow was going to be an awful day. He kept eating slowly, slurping the noodles loudly. In front of him was the image of a protector, salvation in the shape of a man, but this man was unwilling to help the boy. He felt betrayed by his own father. The man tore a piece off the baguette and began chewing like a goat while hundreds of crumbs, heightened and illuminated by the moment, fell and adorned his plate, the table and most likely his lap. The boy was disgusted at every action. These feelings only manifested when he felt people were not who he thought they were. Nor were they who *they said* they were. He was hungry yet the act of staring hatefully was more important and more time consuming. He noticed his anger was palpable but not attention grabbing so his fork played the most excruciating music against the plate.

"That's enough!" said a tormented man, "I had to do it, they had to it" as he pointed at his wife and daughter, "my father had to it, the rest of the world and now you!"

The boy was now angered not by tomorrow but by the fact that this was expected of him, as many things before. He refused to give in.

"I don't want to go to school!"

Trying to hold the man back from screaming even louder, the mother put her utensils down upon her mat and turned to her left where the boy was now crossing his arms again, bowing his head and fighting angry tears with squinting his eyes. She grabbed him by the shoulders and turned him her way. With one swift motion she lifted his chin with one hand and with the other removed the hair from his forehead and kissed him gently on it.

"Mi amor, you need to understand that we all have to go to school. That's how we learn and become adults."

"But mom—"

"I know honey, I know. But really, I promise you there's nothing to fear. You'll be able to draw and play while you make loads and loads of friends. First days at school are intimidating, but you will be just fine. You want to learn, don't you?"

The boy, no longer protesting looked into her welcoming, brown eyes and softened his strained face. The woman now smiling and with open brows stared at her husband with a stern look that told him *that is how you do it.* He rolled his blue-eyes at the entire table and kept rolling the spaghetti noodles around his fork pressed against a large spoon. The table fell silent with the only noise coming from the plates and at times from throats resisting the food coming downward. The boy began to eat slowly still questioning the situation. He was trying to find another way to resist this. Before he had a chance to find an eloquent debate somebody else spoke.

"Hey little buddy, I know how you feel. The first time I went to school *ever,* I was petrified! I didn't want to be in there with those dirty little strangers. But it wasn't that bad. And eventually, you become friends with them. Year after year it gets better, once you know other kids. The moment you overcome the fear of new people, you are fine. It really is so much fun."

His older sister meant well. The boy appreciated the concern from his allies and although still nervous he became more calm. The main concern spiraling over and over again in his head was the fact that he at times felt no protection from his father. It was always what was expected of him. What he was supposed to do for another person's sake or even amusement. Learn this, do this, go here, be this. *NO!* He thought. Enough with that, he needed to feel like the image of what to be was at his side. The man seemed to soften up until he was done with his meal. He quickly scrapped his mouth with a napkin. His mustache made a funky noise caused by the friction and the boy looked up. He then put his silverware upon the finished plate and scolding the boy, stood up and walked into the kitchen were ceramic was heard hitting the metal of the sink and the water spilling loudly over them. The boy knew it was also his fault, for ever questioning his father as he often did. But he thought of himself instead. *I'm scared, not him.*

The young girl thanked her mother for supper and stood up, grabbing other things from the table and taking them away. While this happened the mother put her fork upon her unfinished meal and began picking up too. She didn't want to sit while the girl cleaned up. She walked into the kitchen and you could hear the girls cleaning the dishes and putting away the leftovers. It was always the same scene. Father and daughter done before anyone else and though she was hardly ever done, mother cleaned up and made sure everything was taken care of. Lastly, the boy still fidgeting with the food before he was ever done. Sometimes it could have been thirty minutes after everyone was done before he had finally taken the time to finish his own meal.

"God? Hi, mmm, I wanted to ask you something. I know tomorrow is going to be frightening, but I ask you for something else. Give me protection against the world. Give me emotional support from the ones I love. No matter the situation, let me know I'm taken care of. Amen."

Amid sleep and being awake the boy opened his eyes while hearing whispers. His right eye opened and a hazy silhouette appeared. In fright to what looked like a zombie-scarecrow head dangling from above him, his other eye followed and his body clammed toward the wall behind him while he uttered a low and quick *AHH.* Laughter followed from the bodiless head as the boy's eyes recognized his sister's head looking at him upside down from her bunk bed.

"Hehe Shh, just checking on you. I know tomorrow is a big day, I want you to know everything will be okay. Rest up and we'll be ready for tomorrow. Okay? Love you, goodnight."

His eyes came back to their resting position once he tucked himself again to be able to rest, just like his sister had suggested. Sure, he thought, it was easy for her to say. She had been going to school for a while now. Being four years older than him made it easier for her situation, going back to a school filled with friends, good memories and a clear idea of what the hell they did in this place. Yes, he wanted to learn and prop up to become a responsible adult, but what did it take to do so? And why should he be worried about this if he is just a child?

"Good morning!"

"Morning mom," said the boy early in the morning.

"I'm surprised you are awake this early. On your first day of school, I'm proud of you." She said this while still multi-tasking in the kitchen. Making coffee, getting breakfast together and walking in and out from the kitchen toward the laundry room. Once she stayed in the kitchen for good, he realized she was also making his sister's and his own lunch for school.

"I didn't really sleep well and you and dad being awake woke me up. Hmm, can you tell me why those things you are packing the food in are called lunch boxes? In fact why is it called lunch when it's clear that ten or eleven o'clock in the morning is not lunch time in anyone's mind?"

Puzzled but amused, his mother cocked her head and looked to his direction. "Well, I guess it has to do with the idea of eating period."

"So?"

"Well, you drink coffee in the morning, right?"

"Yes?"

"Well, then why would you need another breakfast? Maybe it goes in the order of eating."

"So, when I come home after school and eat lunch here, it's actually not lunch but what, dinner?"

"Well, how about it's more of a snack than a lunch?"

"So I have two lunches, by the sake of the name, but one is smaller than the other one so it becomes a snack?"

"Yes, that's it."

"This school business is going to be very difficult, isn't it?"

Closing the kid's lunches and moving the boxes toward the table, his mother squatted next to his chair and held his head. "Honey, it is only difficult if you think it is. It's only difficult if you make it difficult. Remember that things are just what you make them be. School is fun if you get into it. I'm sure you don't know it now, but you will come later today with loads of stories of kids you met and played with. Just go with a positive attitude and great things will come. Now," said she standing up and walking toward a plate she had created "I know you need some energy today, so I thought I'd give you this for choice."

"Yummy!" The boy's eyes looked like two sunny side up eggs looking at the plate. The plate contained two varieties of cereal, a beefy sandwich and his favorite.

"Yes, those cookies are yours, as long as you eat the sandwich or the healthy cereals. Balance son, balance."

He could have looked disappointed but he eyed the cookies instead. The round treats had chunks of chocolate that you could see from space. He bit into the sandwich mercifully and kept looking toward his goal. Once three quarters of the sandwich were gone, he excused himself and stood up "I need to go get ready" he said to his mom and then when she turned away to the stove he snuck three cookies as he left.

Once in his room, the one he shared with his sister, he saw her sitting on his bed tying up her shoes. He walked up to her and stood quietly looking down at her.

"Good morning! Oh! Gross! Please don't get crumbs all over my uniform."

He looked at her and saw the white t-shirt adorned with the school's symbol sewed on the left side of her chest.

"Do you like it?"

"When do I get to use the white shirts? Oh, yes, you look fine."

"Well, you wear the yellow shirts until first grade, that's when you switch. Then comes white, then blue, then brown."

"Blue?"

"Yep. Blue. But that's a while from now. Enjoy the yellow while you can."

The boy went toward the closet where the night before his mother had hung his new blue jeans and his freshly bought yellow t-shirt. His mom had also sewed the symbol upon the left part of the chest. It read *School of the Guardian Angel.* He thought whether he had one and if he did, would the angel have to get fired. He still didn't want to go. But he decided he would, at least to go, hate it, then come back and say *Told you so!* Specially to his father, the reason why he was still bitter. He walked into the bathroom and while his sister tied his shoe laces he brushed his teeth.

Strokes went and came. Finally he spit out white foam inside the sink and opened the faucet. The water splashed a bit hard and his sister pulled his left leg.

"Eww! You got toothpaste on my hair dummy."

"Sorry" said he amid laughs. But not too funnily, since he didn't want to lose an ally. Specially not today.

The two of them walked out one behind the other as their mother said goodbye with kisses and waves. Their father was finishing a cigarette leaning against the driver's door of the red vehicle. He had been outside warming up the car, smoking and enjoying the cool breeze that was part of the darkened mornings. He waved toward his wife and without saying anything but "finally" he got in the car and since the gates were already open he sat with his head turned all the way trying to see behind the car and just waiting for the kids to be safely inside. The last door closed and the car sped backward. "Just hope we are not late."

He had a way of making a crappy day seem worse. Not only was the boy petrified of his first day but now was creating plenty of ulcers thinking about being late and being the last one to walk in a room full of strange kids. *Thanks dad*, he thought.

From the outside the school didn't seem as threatening, but it felt that way. There were pinkish walls that ended by the graffiti of a happy school land with boys and girls ever so happy, flying books and notebooks, smiling pencils and friendly pens, erasers that took all the pain away and happy angel-like adults. The boy questioned them and figured they were supposed to be the teachers. The car stopped and he heard a screeching noise, he saw his father let go of the emergency break and turn the car off.

"Okay. Get out, it's time."

"See, not so bad, right?" His sister said.

"Yeh, we're not inside the place yet!"

"Oh, come on!"

Of course traffic was nonexisting and although his father wanted to make it seem otherwise, there was barely anyone there. Some teachers and some poor little kids, most likely sons and daughters of the teachers who were early. His father was walking as if the day was gone and time was to be terminated. Always fast, always hurrying, always go go go! They walked through the entire school as if to make the boy feel safe. Showing him the main office, where if anything were to go wrong, he could tell somebody or use the phone to call home. Then, they made sure he knew the number by heart. Which he recited with a sarcastic tone. They showed him the cantina, the soccer fields, the library and the side of the school which pertained to the high schoolers. They came into the open space that was for the elementary school kids. This area was also shared by the younger kids, just like him. The open space seemed limitless. And then the walking stopped. His sister let go of his hand and together with the father they turned to look at him.

"This is it!" The father looked around aimlessly.

"Okay, so I need to go to my classroom, but I will be coming by here to see you at recess, okay? I love you! Be good!" And his sister galloping toward her designated area kissed him on the cheek and disappeared into the distance. This meant he was left alone with his father. He turned to look at him through the now shining sunlight. Squinting he made peace with the idea of making his most wanted ally, right then and there.

"Dad?"

"Yes?"

"I'm sorry about fearing this, I will be good I promise."

"You're okay son, no worries."

He grabbed his son's tiny little hand and ended up letting the boy grab his index finger with his entire hand. They walked toward the classroom and the boy began seeing kids more clearly. They kept coming in and there were many of them already inside. It seemed this was a very important day indeed. He saw everyone's parents, one or another, holding their kids. Introducing them to the teacher, the toys, the kids and prepping them for the rest of their lives it felt like. After seeing that he felt less threatened but still quite suspicious. They sat down and his father removed his tiny book bag and placed it on a desk filled with other much more colorful ones. Then he tried to take the lunch box, but the boy decided that his fuel was to stay with him at all times. He held onto the handle and paced around the small area. Around his father, he looked at the toys and took in the smell of foreign. He was still suspicious and the fact that a boy was crying and pleading for his mother to take him away did not help. The dark boy had streams washing down his round face. He held onto the gates fierce fully without quieting down. The sight made the boy swallow coldly behind his father's legs.

"Hey, hey, don't worry! He's just afraid like you are, he just decided to cry."

"What if there is something scary in here! Is there? Dad?!"

"Haha, no son, there isn't anything to be afraid of."

"Don't lie dad! Is there?"

"I wouldn't lie to you son. Look around. See anything scary?"

The boy looked at the one crying with sarcastic eyes and the father agreed, "Okay, anything else but the kid?"

"I guess not."

"Okay, come on, you'll do fine. The kids will be great and you'll do all kinds of things."

A second later the teacher came closer and introduced herself.

"You know sir, if you chose, like many other parents, you can stay as long as you'd like. It is a hard transition sometimes. Even if you aren't in the classroom but on school grounds, you could."

The father looked suspiciously uncomfortable at the request but smiled nonetheless.

"Thank you."

"Well then, very nice to finally meet *you*. I know we will have loads of fun! See you later, take care sir." The teacher walked toward another parent and did it all again.

"Great! You can stay with me."

"Well," said the father questioning his own intent.

"Please, can you? I'm still not buying this. Plus, if you say there's nothing to fear, why wouldn't you stay?"

"Hey buddy, you need to be independent."

"What is that?"

"Well, you need to learn to be on your on sometimes."

"Why?"

"Because someday you might be in a situation were there won't be a person and you need to be okay with that."

"What? How about you and mom? You wouldn't leave me alone, right?!"

"No, no, that's not what I mean."

"Can you please stay?"

"Come on, just come sit here with me and let's see people walk in."

The boy and his father sat upon a wooden table that stood two feet tall at most. Each chair was of a different pigment. Each leg was of a different pigment. Once you looked at it over and over it was okay but to begin with the combination of yellow, pink, orange, green, red and blue did give out headaches like candy. They saw a girl with her father walk in. She had two pony tails on each side of her head and had the brightest, most pink book bag ever seen with a picture of Barbie in the middle of it. She seemed ready, willing and able to cope with this wretched day. She took her father by his long shirt and pulled him through the crowds of others up until where she felt comfortable. They sat. Then he saw a pair of boys, friends perhaps, walking inside with their own toys in hand and shouting silly boy sayings until an old man grabbed a hold of them and told them to quiet down. They did, momentarily, then they ran outside screaming again. He laughed once he saw the old man run outside to get them.

The classroom was now pretty full and he began to question what they did here that was so fun and helpful. His father took a hard and long look at the watch across his left wrist and let his right hand move through his thick hair.

"Okay pal, I need, I need to pee."

"Oh, okay."

"I'll be right back."

"I'll go with you."

"No, no, stay here, I'll be a minute."

"I don't want to stay here by myself."

"Okay, come here," he let his son follow toward the gates that surrounded the classroom. "You can stand right here and you can see me. See those doors right there? It's not far away, is it? I'll be right back." He kissed the boy's forehead and started walking. The boy stood looking past the gates and saw his father wave twice on the way to the doors of the bathroom.

A couple of minutes passed and the boy was still by the gates. He had counted all the banks outside by the big oak tree. He had counted from left to right, from right to left, by color. Then he counted the bars across that made up the gates. It seemed like a good idea, he thought, to paint each bar a different color. If he moved his eyes quickly, he could sense the point. Most likely to weaken the senses, the mind and keep everyone prisoner inside this classroom. What awful colors, just like that table. He turned to look at it as if it had to feel ashamed of itself.

Other minutes passed and he sat by the gates. The kids inside were making loads of noise but he couldn't hear them. He was now singing to himself. He tapped his fingers one at a time upon the metal bars. Up and down, down and up. Left to right, right to left. He looked at the doors, they were motionless. He figured there was a line inside. *Boy, everybody is peeing today.* He thought it was funny that nobody else seemed to be exiting the bathroom, or for that matter, going in it. He started to worry.

The teacher came toward him and squatted on his right side.

"Hello! Would you prefer to come over here with the others? You can introduce yourself, you don't have to be afraid. I can help you."

"That's okay. I can do that with my father."

"Where is he darling?"

"He'll be right back."

"Honey, I think he left. Didn't he?"

"No! He is in the bathroom. I'm waiting for him."

"Are you sure?"

"Yes! He went to the bathroom right through those doors and he'll be right back."

"Honey, that's not the bathroom now come on, if you want to make today a success you need to come into the group and not think of yourself as being alone. Your father will come get you later, come with me."

"No! He's coming!"

As she tried to hold his hand, he stood and pushed her away. He ran out of the classroom toward the doors and as he got closer to it an arm grabbed him by the shoulder.

"Hey! You cannot run out of the room like that! You hear me?! Come back with me."

"He's in there" and as he pointed with his other arm and head, he looked through the door and saw trash bags inside. "What is that?"

"That's the trash deposit son, not a bathroom. Now, come with me."

He tugged away slowly and pulling the teacher with his tiny body he got even closer to it until he pushed the door and saw another door that was opened that led to the street. He saw cars parked on either side of the street and realized that it wasn't a bathroom after all. His disappointment let him lose his strength when the teacher pulled him back toward the classroom and locked the gates. She sighed and looked into his eyes.

"I know you are afraid, but there is nothing to fear. Just think about your father picking you up at the end of the day. He said he would come and he wouldn't lie to you, would he?"

She stood up and walked away. His eyes became red with anger. There were streams of wrath striking one at a time down his heaving cheeks. He grabbed the gates with his left hand and with the right one found and held tightly to his lunch box. He had remembered his mother working on his meal and he wouldn't let it out of his sight. It was respect toward her. Now he looked out toward the distance, the banks, the trees, it all seemed so far away. His tears made everything seem gloomy even when thinking about that lying graffiti.

He looked down and his ears began opening up again, letting life around him be noticed. He heard a cry he had heard before. He saw the dark child, like him, holding onto the metal bars and still crying, less than before, but with heavier incentive. He turned away from the other child and realized his mother had left *him*. What a day for the two. Standing there, alone, in a prison cell. Taken there by loved ones. Deceivers. Liars. Tears kept falling as he realized he had learned his first lesson. The first day of school was the final day of trust. The bell rang and the day had just begun.

Bad Influence

Dark brown parcels of wood staring back. Wonderful sight, first thing in the morning. The bunk bed was rather comfortable, but scary if you slept on the bottom one. My sister and I used to have moments through the year when we would decide change was necessary. The trick about sleeping underneath another bed was just, to sleep and do it. The idea of already being on the floor when you got off the bed sounded better than the other choice. Living on the upside of the beds, meant climbing down a ladder early in the morning, which, honestly, could be very dangerous. Stupid idea, it was. And stupid us, that thought it was plainly amusing. Kids climbing ladders, wooden at that, first thing in the morning. Nonsense. I had a moment when I appreciated my life more than commodity, and I slept on the top mattress, although, it gave me hernias from trying to be quiet in the middle of the night, trying to get down to go take a wee and not wake the older sister. Now, opening my little hazel eyes and watching hazy wooden parcels wasn't too bad. My last trick was to open my eyes and run out from underneath. It was exhausting, but it meant fast escape and a little exercise along the way.

Light brown, I locked the door behind me. The ceramic tiles were frozen against my feet. Even in the tropic, you can have such a scene. Nonsense. The air conditioning was maintained on at all times in the bedroom, and since our bathroom was attached to it, it retained a part of the cold. Mostly in the tile temperature. Standing over the big bowl, I pulled down my pants and held onto lazily with one hand and rubbed my sleep-tight eyes. The warm breeze caressed my skin. What a mind trick, temperature in the morning. It doesn't matter when, where or why, but the body is always slow in adjusting. Although this is from personal experience, maybe I should get checked. The sink rested right underneath my chin, and the mirror was too tall for me to see the top of my hair, so with that, I put paste on my brush and bobbed my head sideways for entertainment. Funny how a mirror, self-image, can be so amusing. Not having so, is truly missed. Big rinse, big spit. The blue sink had snowflakes melting down to the core. There were bubbles like an ocean filled with soap. The water ran down ending it, and then a big rub against my sleeve.

Once I exited the bathroom, slightly more awake, I made my bed. I fluffed my pillow, and then walked back. With an accomplished grin, I crossed my arms and contemplated at my beautifully made bed. With all honesty, my approval was mostly for the sheets and their design, but I made it pretty well too. A big part of the sheets was purple, and then it had different sized orange squares with each individual Ninja Turtle. It was my favorite, and oh, so comfortable. My night stand looked crowded, but I figured I would take care of it later. I was thirsty, that was more important. I stood still for a second, and yawned at the day, *welcome new day*. After lowering my arms to my sides, I slipped my right hand in the back of my pants and scratched mercilessly at my right butt cheek. *Aah. Heaven.* The room made me cold again, so I remembered my thirst. Once more, light brown, and the room door was closed.

Another blow against my skin, the air outside of the bedroom was dry, making me cough slightly. The warmth gave me back the energy that the bedroom chill had taken away. Rubbing my arms up and down, I helped my body get used to it. The kitchen was barely five steps away from our bedroom, so I entered. I stopped at the sight, and rolled my eyes without moving them. Maybe it was just the intent that I felt, but it was something that was expected on some level. Disappointment has that magnitude. Being able to be wanted, to be able to look life in the eyes and say "Guess what? I've won!" The sad part of that whole exchange is that, indeed one was right about being disappointed, but that clearly gives life another victory. Human greed for victory. Nonsense. To my disbelief, I was born to expect this. I grew up to expect this. I was taught to understand it. And bluntly, taught to accept it and expect it. Still half asleep, I guess the bathroom and temperature shifts were no match for my need to rest, I walked slowly trying not to get my foot cut open. There was a clean glass at my reach, which I grabbed and placed under the faucet of the kitchen sink and let the water pour. The water felt great against my lips, they were still glued with saliva in the corners. The lukewarm water felt great playing with my tongue, with my gums and burning with pleasure down my throat. With a large sigh, I put the glass down and looking at the sight, emotionless, I wiped a tear with my sleeve and walked away.

The bedroom was quiet, and I didn't even feel the chill this time, I was on a mission. I looked up above and saw the sheets bulking to the side and felt bad about wanting her awake. Climbing the wooden ladder, I extended my arm and poked the sheets. Instead of feeling a body moving, the sheets went all the way down, and folded in showing my sister was either shrunk into oblivion or not sleeping. How thick is the feeling of stupid, specially when I had been going around the house this whole time, thinking my sister was asleep. I was a solid sleeper, but great for waking early. Always had, walking around the house before everybody would be even considering it, feeling the heaviness of the early morning, when the day is up, but everybody is still holding on to their dreams. On the weekends, when we all give ourselves a chance to sleep in, I tended to go into my parents bedroom, afraid of such early morning heaviness and running to be rescued. Their big, puffy blanket would usually create a cataract at the foot of the bed, letting me create a bed there. Close enough to them, but not waking them to ruin the moment of their young coming in their bedroom and waking them up. But not today.

I walked downward and kept on searching. My first instinct was to go to the front of the house and look out of the window to check on our two cars. Maybe knowing my surroundings before I walked into something I wasn't expecting, would give me the lead on what was going on. The white curtain caressed my head and almost wrapped me inside completely. I lifted the metal bar and the slits of glass went from vertical to horizontal, and the driveway was illuminated by the sun. There was only one vehicle, my mother's. I let the curtain fall over the window, and let my head put the puzzle together. *This makes more sense, of course.* I turned and the entire house was dark. Funny how the true early mornings are more scary than the latest, darkest nights. The clock against the wall in the living room said six thirteen. I braved the darker inward walk and slowly crept closely to my parent's bedroom door, it was closed, so I chose to inspect further. Instead of staying there, I walked into the guest bedroom in the back of the house, and looked out that window. The patio looked dead, as did our two dogs. I gasped loudly until I saw their bellies rise and drop with each breath. Suddenly, Mickey, the boy, lifted his head erect, and then laid back down, eventually dropping sideways. Not even the dogs were awake, barking as usual. It was way too early, and no matter what happened, they were taking their precious time sleeping. *Oh, yeh, what did happen?*

My warm earlobe touched the wood and I tried to listen, nothing really came out. After that moment, I began to worry. Opening the door quietly and silently, I let some cold air out and with it came a sob. The door was slowly closed again, and I moved to the spot that would allow me to listen without a problem. I sat on my bed and looked at my night stand, and I grabbed all of the crap upon it and threw it on my bed, the air vent that connected my parent's bedroom and ours was brilliant. It was right beside my night stand and it connected me to my parent's small hallway that started their room. This had a wonderful echo effect that resonated magnificently against my readily ears. The sobbing was stronger and I was trying to figure out what it was, without making a bigger fuss about it. It's always good to be prepared, and although genuine emotions are always nice, I preferred knowing and then if being confronted about hearing something or being worried and scared, I would act indifferently. Come to find out, my mother was the one crying, I expected nothing less, but this knowledge burned deep inside my stomach and made my fists tighten.

The talking was inaudible, most likely being whispered to an extreme in the furthest point of the room, maybe even the master bathroom. *Crap.* I tried my best, but I could only hear the same thing over and over. I waited, but instead I heard a body walking out of the room and I wanted to be in bed, but all of my things were thrown on top of it. Instead, I had to make myself seem occupied. Our bedroom door opened and with me looking up, I grabbed my big Aladdin coin can, and placed it on the furthest corner of my night stand. I grabbed the end of my sleeve and I rubbed it on it, as if dusting.

"Hey, how long have you been awake?"

"Oh, hey, I didn't see you standing there. Not too long." I looked into my sister's green eyes with certainty and added, "I was wondering where you were."

"What are you doing?"

"Oh, you know, it was bothering me, all these things crowding in the corner of my eye, so I chose to clean up a bit and be more organized." Her eyes pierced the side of my head as I tried to keep going with my farce. A second body was heard exiting my parent's room and while I looked up, the green specs were still questioning my actions. A door opened and my sister gave a small sideways smile out of ours and she looked down again.

"You didn't hear anything?" I nodded sideways. "Well, whatever, I doubt it, but please don't be a handful today, mom is tired, okay?" I nodded upward this time. She exited it and I blurted out "What happened in the kitchen?" I quickly realized, after she never came back inside the room, that I was whispering the whole time.

There were brushing sounds coming from the kitchen. From outside of it I could see my mom's behind, as she bent over to clean up the mess. There were screws and bolts all over the floor. There was a large piece of wood close to the doorway that had fallen of the table. The kitchen table itself was resting diagonally against the wall, broken off from where it was being held before, and there were napkins, a bread basket, among other things scattered as well. Mother brushed and sniffled through each stroke. The light from outside was now more apparent, and it made the entire scene even more realistic. There was no escaping it now. Before, I could have fallen asleep and woken up after they had cleaned up. But now, my nose was just as powdered as everybody else's. She turned still brushing and saw me standing there. Her first reaction was to feel sorry for me. Her facial expressions said it all. But as mom would do, she forced a smile through her red, puffy eyes.

"What are you doing awake, huh? Enjoy your Saturday, go to sleep."

We both stood in silent. She brushed, and I refused to accept her proposal.

"Where's everybody?" I just wanted to ask about my sister, but let it slip out that way. Which in the long run, would be more beneficiary.

"Your sister is outside getting the big trash bags and the large garbage bin."

My sister happened to walk at that moment with a black, plastic bag and looked down at me, making sure I was behaving and not asking the wrong questions.

"And your father is, out."

My sister's green eyes could have killed me, now knowing I did ask the wrong question.

"He had to do some things before he got into work, he should be home after that. You know, at the usual two o'clock," she kept herself busy and only made eye contact at the end of every seventh word, "then, we will have lunch. You guys can help me once I figure out what we are having."

That was weird in itself, as we usually didn't cook on Saturdays. Since we went to our grandparent's house on Sunday for lunch, and cooked, we always had takeout on Saturdays. Mother knew her answer was fishy, but it was the best thing that occurred to her at the moment, without being too open but not lying about the situation.

"Hey, why don't you help cleaning, please." My sister scorned me.

"No no. At least put some shoes on if you're going to be in here. I don't want you walking on something. Go put some shoes on." My mother added.

"**D**ad!!" I ran inside the house trying to find him.

"What's with the racket? What?"

"Dad, can you come outside? We stopped the ice cream man and we want to get some. Please?"

"Alright." Father wiped his hands with the kitchen towel, and threw it upon the counter. I followed him inside of his bedroom to make sure he was coming right behind me. Father picked his wallet out of a pair of jeans folded upon a chair. He looked at me. "Go! I'm right behind you." I ran out of the house and he came behind me. My sister and the neighborhood kids were all over the small ice cream cart waving bills and screaming over each other. Most of the kids were now walking away stuffing their faces, my sister included. Because I was smaller than the rest, father picked me up and I was able to look inside of it. After I reached it, I picked a purple triangle. It was my favorite, as it had a ball of gum at the bottom of it. It was like two treats at once. Father put me down on the ground and I moved away excitedly. We walked back into our front garden and sat under the shade. The summer was always horrible. If it could get any hotter, it would. My father waved goodbye to the ice cream man and came in, locking the surrounding gate. He kept walking and I realized he had gotten one for himself. I smiled at the sight. He saw me do so and smiled back.

"What? Can't get one now?"

He was wearing blue shorts and a white tank top. He stood there, sweating like a pig, and devouring his treat. My sister stood up and began jumping up and down around the grass, I figured it was to get cooler. On the other hand, she was that type of girl. Absent at times when she felt a natural need to dance and do ballet. The sun scratched me, even in the shade, it was tremendously hateful. I never did like the sun that much. My fair skin hissed back, and pushed my entire body further back.

"How is it?"

"Good, dad, thank you."

"You want to play football?"

"No, dad, thank you."

"Okay."

Another attempt was turned down as I wasn't feeling like making the effort. It did excite me that he asked, wanting to spend time with me. It was as if I was playing hard to get with my own father. Something we both did for years. Finally, father ended up with a wooden stick, he laughed as he read the riddle written on it, and walked inside. Closing the door. I was still sitting, on my own, and I could hear the bells from the ice cream cart. There were no clouds across the sunny sky, and I just sweat the sweetness through each pale pore.

"Are you okay?" I turned up and looked at her. I was laying on the bedroom floor watching television. By the time I had put my shoes on, the two of them had finished cleaning, and after we all had some breakfast, I went outside with the dogs, then came in to watch cartoons and the girls went all over the house doing things that exhausted me just by the thought. My sister seemed concerned, slouching down above me and placing her open palm on top of my back. I didn't know what to say, I didn't really know what was going on. In other words, I was angry, as usual, with the fact of insinuation alone, without any solid proof or reason.

"Dad is not feeling well today. They had a rough night."

"I didn't hear anything."

"It was very late."

"Is that what happened to the table? He broke it?"

She nodded in agreement. "He should be fine after he gets off work and comes home to eat. I think mom is showering so that we can start making lunch." She tickled me when she said this as to build some type of amusement within me, but I stayed still.

"That's fine. I bet he'll feel bad about the table. He'll be embarrassed."

"Well, if that's the case," she added, "we'll deal with it then."

"Yes, you're right. I just hope he's not going to be the same when he comes." I turned back to the television and I felt her hand stay put for a couple of seconds. Then, I knew she was fearing the same. She said nothing else, stood up, and went out of the room.

All we had to do was wait. He worked until roughly two in the afternoon on Saturdays, but I just felt the day was different. In fact, the hours piled on, and after my sister helped my mom cook, the three of us ate, at three fifteen. My mother had called the office after two o'clock. Of course, there was no answer. Then, she called his personal phone. Nothing. She did this for a while, until she began to worry and started calling outward within his networking circle.

"Yes, hi Nino, how are you today? Yes, yes. Listen, has he stopped by there today? He did? An hour ago? Okay, well, thank you Nino, goodbye." Mother put the phone down and exhaled with aggravation.

"Yes, I have tried his number, but he was supposed to be home after work and it is, now, way passed it. Yes, yes, I'll be calm, just call me if you hear or see him, okay?"

"At what time did you see him today? He left work an hour early? Oh, okay. Did you know where he was heading? No."

By nine o'clock my mother had called everybody she could think of. Work related, neighborhood related, or weekend related. Nothing. I had seen her become even more nervous than she previously had been. I heard some of the calls, but my sister kept me inside of the room. Finally, I went out in the silence, and my sister was holding my mother's hand as they both were sitting at the table. They saw me walk out, and my mother had that sideways smile again, but this time tears were running down and she began weeping. I sat to her other side and grabbed her other hand.

"I'm sorry, my babies. I don't like that you see me crying. Everything will be okay, you know?"

"It's okay mom, we all cry sometimes." She looked at me and kissed me on the cheek, wetting me with her tears. "That's true baby."

"Is dad coming back?"

"Yes."

"Is he okay?"

"Honey, dad is *not* okay. He is having some trouble." She looked at both of us and her sweet tone was replaced by seriousness.

"Daddy is kinda sick. You know, he has a lot on his mind. Some problems that go way back, years ago, that have nothing to do with you, or you, and they make him very sad. Just know he's not mad at you nor is he trying to make you worried. If you can, please, when he gets home, try to show him some love. Be kind and try to be well behaved."

As soon as her last word ended, the gate could be heard being opened outside. It slammed. The car could be heard revving, then stopping, and the door close. It slammed. The three of us sat there, on the dinning room table, petrified. Keys were heard and the front door opened. We were motionless and my mother stood up. Father came in dragging himself and limping sideways. I knew he'd be drunk. Almost positive that this was the same sight last night. But instead of him being gone the whole day and then walking in, he did it in the comfort ability of his own home. With the most powerful disappointment, I looked life in the eyes and reminded her I had won. Then a tear rolled down and I was slapped in the face by life itself. *No, I'm sorry to tell you, I have won. Again.*

Father began shouting and my sister, with one quick motion, lifted me by grabbing my arm and dragged me into the bedroom and closed the door. It was both a brave and a cowardly move. Taking me in, to keep me from harm, but leaving mother behind. I was always mad at that idea. As if her duty was to take such position. Screams were heard for too long as they moved around the house. I heard the kitchen table slam. Poor thing, as if it wasn't already beat to a pulp. I looked at the clock inside the bedroom, it was ten thirty. My sister and I stayed inside our room, trying to listen. They eventually moved to the bedroom, where he was still screaming at her, incoherently, and we could hear it all. He suddenly stopped, and there was a tremendous silence. It scared us for a bit, but eventually, their silence, became our silence and we were falling asleep. I know I did, waking up later on not knowing what I had missed. Nothing, apparently, except for my father crying. He was sobbing like a child for a while, and after being awake, I heard him for at least thirty minutes. I looked at the clock up above, twelve twenty-two in the morning.

There's something disgusting about eavesdropping, specially when you can't help but. A necessity that should never be. What made it worse for me, was the sobbing. It broke my heart into pieces, and it just kept me on edge. Hearing somebody cry, whether you know the person nor if you care for that person, it tears you apart. An exhausting session of disgusting, necessary habits. At one point, it turned up again, and his cries became an elongation of his self-exorcism. We heard mom walk out, and walk into our room crying and asking us to follow her. She led us to her room, where just by what we had just heard, and simple fright, began crying as we got closer and closer to our father.

He sat there, hunching over himself, barely breathing, in the most unbearable pain. His arms were limp and his fair skin was red all over. His body was exhausted. When I walked in, I realized the wall was punctured, and father's right hand had blood on it. Mom told him we were there and he cried harder, louder. He was obviously embarrassed, and mother worked on both terms. Wanting him to be sorry to us, yet make us be grateful to him and show him our love. Now the four bodies crying, the kids hugged their father. He was reluctant to hug back, but eventually did, lovingly. Apologetically crying, he mumbled sorry to everybody and we hugged him tighter.

I never did care what had happened, knowing my father and I had difficulties. Knowing that father was intricate and complicated. And just remembering the times when he wasn't like this. Not breaking things, not drunk, not absent, not screaming, not angry, not sad, not crying, but the best father I ever could ask for.

"So, what do you think they do all night?"

"Well, I'm guessing they don't sleep then, do they? I mean, they must be smart about their options and work when they're not stepped on. At night, they can check out the surroundings and find food easily without trouble."

"Maybe they do, but the night time is harder to search in, and I don't think ants have lamps or lanterns. haha"

"Yeh, but don't we all find ways to accommodate ourselves? Dad, they need to be smart. I think they have spies during the day, and then they know where the food is and that we are all sleeping. Isn't the night time when most things happen?"

"I wouldn't know, I sleep at night. But I'll tell you this, whenever you and I are both awake in the middle of the night, I bet we'll know how it feels to be spies."

"Promise?"

"Promise."

The moonlight led the path and the ants marched underneath the stars.

Sweet

You're More Than Welcome to Join Me

"**H**ey buddy," The young boy fluttered his sleepy eyes and rubbed them fighting the harsh light biting back at him. Instead of answering, he pulled his sheets over his head and murmured to himself. Laughing, the boy's father sat on the side of the bed and looking at the clock on the nightstand, which read 9:30 am, he removed the sheets and pressed on with excitement.

"Come on sleepy, it is time to wake up already."

"Why?" The boy bit back.

"Well, because it's a beautiful day and you've slept enough." The father said lovingly.

"Says who?" Said the boy still irritated.

"Alright, come on" his face already changing from nice to something else, "you need to get up now."

The father stood up and while on his feet, he removed all of the covering sheets, bundled them up and held them against his chest. The boy angered, refused to look up and kneeled face down holding onto the pillow. He tried to keep it going, but he was now awake. Rapidly, he turned his head up and snared at his father. Angrily, he stood up and stamped his little feet toward the bathroom, where he slammed the door. The older man stood in silence and threw the sheets on top of the bed, leaving the bedroom.

The wooden door opened slightly and the boy peeked out of it checking that his father was gone. In one big stretch, he sprung toward the bed and wrapped himself with the ball of sheets and covers. With his head sticking out, the boy laid back realizing that his attitude toward his father was not getting better as he sometimes hoped it would or could. There was an instant of remorse but the boy quickly shot that out of his heart as he felt it harden by the mere thought of his father and his behavior that although was positive and trying, was mainly hurtful and unpredictable. Thinking angrily he fell back asleep and clung to the sheets.

Outside the bedroom, the father paced from the kitchen toward the master bedroom, then past the living room to the front porch. The man, visibly distressed, grabbed a hold of the garden hose and watered plant by plant.

"Mehl?" A voice barely resonated and began getting louder. "Mehl! Where are you?"

"Julia, I'm out here," yelled Mehl.

"Oh, watering the plants, how nice," she got close and resting her petite hands on his shoulder, she kissed him gently on the lips. Mehl obliged.

"Remember that we have to leave by," Julia looked at her watch, "six-thirty to get to the party on time."

"That's fine."

"Okay, great. I'll be leaving momentarily. After I go to the store, I'll be stopping by mother's house to drop some things off. Just make sure that Anthony doesn't do anything that gets him too dirty, or at least keep an eye on him."

"Sure." Mehl didn't look at Julia and kept answering without intent, but more as a reflex.

"Oh, I forgot to ask you, where were you this morning? I barely heard you when you went out."

"Nothing; I was just getting the car checked."

"Oh, okay, great. I'll get my purse and I'll be leaving then."

Julia walked inward and closed the door behind her. Mehl watered the plants and while wetting the pavement momentarily, jerked his left hand which held the hose, as he inserted his right one in his front pocket. From the pocket he removed an insignificantly small, purple lighter. Then, he removed the cigarette being held behind his ear and lit it up, blowing a large cloud and watering the grass once again. The current weather was drying the once green grass which took up most of the patio, on either side to the walkway from the front gate. Mehl allowed the humidity to drench him as his lips, in addition to the heat, warmed his entire body by the suction of the cigarette. Exhaling one last time, he walked toward the valve and turned the water off. Rolling the hose he waved goodbye to Julia, who through the back of the house had entered her car and driven out of the driveway. Mehl looked out waving and as the car disappeared into the distance, held his sides with each hand and tried to remember exactly what she had said previous to departing.

Walking back inside the house he saw Anthony walking past the hallway toward the kitchen and heard him stub one of his toes. "Ouch!" Anthony screamed from afar. Mehl sighed as he wanted to have a good moment with his son, which was hard to come by. Another noise came from the kitchen and out of it came Anthony with a glass of milk. Before he was out of sight again, Mehl tried to say something out loud, but nothing came until he blurted loudly.

"Hey you!" Mehl waited for a response. Anthony walked backward and turned his head slightly to the right and without ever answering he sipped from his glass.

"Now that you are awake, I wanted to give you something." Mehl said trying to excite the boy.

"I got you something," said he as he opened a bag that lied on top of a chair in the dining room. Anthony was visibly excited.

"I got you a nice soccer ball."

"Oh." Anthony's face stretched downward and rolling his eyes just kept drinking his milk.

"No no," reassured Mehl, "you'll like it. Here." Finally, Mehl removed the ball from the bag and presented it to his son.

"Whoa!" the boy excited again put the glass down on top of the dining table and grabbed the ball with tremor. Anthony touched it as if it were made of glass. Surprisingly, this ball was something he wanted not to shatter.

"You like it?" Mehl waited for much wanted approval.

"Each hexagon has a picture on it." Anthony was too mesmerized to look away.

"I know. Each hexagon has an international flag on it. Pretty cool, eh?"

"This is awesome! Where did you get it?"

"Oh, you know, I know people. HAHA" Mehl grabbed the ball from

Anthony and with wide open eyes said "You want to go to the back and play a little?"

After such a wonderful gift, Anthony felt like it was his duty to oblige and go play a little soccer with his father. Deep in his mind he realized that this gift was a way for his father to make him do something he knew Anthony didn't like. That fact irritated him and took a little off the gift. Why would he push himself so harshly upon his son? Why wasn't he trying to do something for the kid for once instead of preparing him to be a carbon copy of whom he wanted as a child? The boy thought about his options, and figured he would be smart about what to do without being hurtful, although if it happened, so be it.

"It's new, dad. Plus, I don't want to wreck the designs on it. I rather put it away so I can appreciate its potential. Thank you." Anthony got close to his father and hugged him. He turned and holding his ball walked toward his bedroom.

"That's good. Take care of it. Let me go ahead and grab one of the ones we have in the patio and I'll wait for you so we can play a little."

The boy's shoulders elevated and he hid the disgust in his face. Seeing his father move made him snap quickly to him.

"No! Wait, I don't really want to right now. I was thinking," he put the ball down and turned to his father who was now in the doorway toward the kitchen "we could go to the pool. The weather is perfect and we can hang out for a little bit."

"I don't want to go get ready for the pool. Come on, let's just play for a little bit."

"I rather not play. I feel like getting in the pool. Yes?"

"No pool for me. Are you sure?"

"Yes," now turning and grabbing the ball again and refusing to try any harder, "I'm in the mood to draw right now and then I'll get ready to go into the pool." Without ever turning at this point and walking into his room, "You're more than welcome to join me."

Anthony got out of the bathroom in his multi colored briefs. A towel wrapped around his head made it fall backward, but he fought it straightening his posture. In front of the closet he stood humming loudly and with his small, left hand scratched his naked belly. Looking up at the hung clothes, he tried to figure out which outfit was the one his mom picked out for him. Finding it, Anthony grabbed it and held it high past his head, to make sure it wasn't touching the floor and laid it on top of the bed. The little, blue dress pants looked goofy, but he liked that about them. Attached to it was a red and white, collar t-shirt. Touching the insides of it, he verified that he approved of the material. The shoes were next to the bed, and although they were somewhat dressy, they were very comfortable when he wore them, and looked mostly casual. Looking over at the entire outfit, Anthony felt good about it. Walking back to the bathroom, he opened a jar above the toilet and removed a q-tip from it. Back in the room, he rubbed it inside each ear, as he liked to be precisely clean. The outfit seemed to be the most exciting idea about the evening. Lamentably, the fact that some of his buddies were going to be there wasn't good enough, as he knew he was going to deal with a lot of crap. Especially because of the silly outfit, the one he loved.

The young boy, already in his socks, meticulously removed the pants from the hanger and slipped them on. The shirt followed and he tucked it inside his pants. Lastly, he walked into each shoe. Making sure he was well put together, he walked to the closet again, without missing a beat. To the left side of it, were hooks holding his belts. The thickest one made it to his hands, perfectly matching his shoes, he slid it trough a loop at a time. Inside the bathroom, he looked into the mirror and allowed his outfit to make sense; it did. Knowing he was done, he grabbed a small cologne bottle, CK One, which his mother gave him and he rolled the bottle all along the sides of his neck and his wrists, just like adults seemed to do.

Completely dressed, the young boy walked out of his room and peeked at his parents', where they were still pacing around. Anthony decided to wait for them in the living room and sat on the sofa. The moonlight shimmered through the open curtains and illuminated the inside of the house in a straight line. From inside the rooms walked the two of them. Excitedly, Julia judged her son's outfit and smiled kissing his small lips.

"Honey, you look great! This is fantastic on you!"

41

"Alright, let's get out of here. We're late as it is." Mehl pushed them out of the door and locked it behind him. Julia and Anthony entered the car and closed their doors. After putting his seatbelt on and checking that their son had too, Mehl looked back and drove the car out of the driveway. The roads were clear and even though he could have easily driven through the couple red lights they hit, Mehl decided to stay put even though no cars were around. At the last light, the car sat there waiting and one that drove up behind it honked at him, later driving around, the driver, a bearded thick man shouted and gestured at them. Julia was appalled, but it made Anthony giggle.

Once at the designated location, Mehl parallel parked the car and the two adults got out of the car. Anthony stayed in, and with one big push, opened the door and slammed it behind him. His ears started to take in the noise little by little, and he could hear the party buzzing across the street. The small apartment complex was a great place for parties. It was made up of a two story building, with four apartments, all owned by the same family. The parking lot was made for at least eight cars, and it was fenced around the front, making the property almost circular.

Walking closer, there were kids running around the lot, tables set up in the back, next to some cars, and the front doors opened to all of the houses, for easy bathroom and kitchen access. The adults were all over, as there was a barbecue going, visibly conquered by the men, and chatter filled the air, as it became thicker and harder to understand.

"Look who made it!" Marco, a close friend of the family greeted them and hugged each individual except the boy.

"How are you little Tony? Daniel and the other kids are around the back, go find them and play." Marco and Mehl walked away as Marco gave the boy's father a bottle of beer and the two laughed and walked toward the others. Julia waved from afar but had realized that Anthony was hurt by the quick dismissal.

"Baby, go over there and have fun, okay? I'll be here and when you get hungry, I'll get you a plate. Okay?" Tenderly, she caressed his hand and walked away greeting Marco's wife and the other mothers. Whose party was this anyway? Anthony couldn't remember, but he got that painful thing in his stomach and couldn't care less about the party's purpose. Turning around, he heard and saw some of the older kids, his age, starting to run and scream around the corner from the back. He smiled to some of them, some he knew, some he didn't, but mostly he was fearful of the state of things. Adults didn't seem to understand that kids' social lives are very complicated. It seemed like everyone felt and acted different depending on the day and whom they were with. Anthony laughed inside his head thinking *That doesn't happen with adults, silly. Why would they understand?*

"Hey Tony, how are you?" Daniel, Marco's son approached his friend, as they were longtime neighbors.

"Hey Dan, I'm okay, you know I'm just—"

"Hey fag." Daniel's cousin, Jean rudely interrupted. "Nice gay outfit. Where did you get It from, your mom?" He laughed and some comments came from the others behind him. "Score!" "Good one!" "Burned!" "What a fag."

"Yes, I got it from her, where else would I? It's not like I have money to buy it. I´m just a kid." Anthony retorted with his quick mouth, not caring about Jean being twice his size and not needing an excuse to use his advantage. At the same time, Daniel snickered and enjoyed the smart-mouth boy.

"You think you're funny?" Jean, did not. "Did you find it funny Dan?" Fearing his older cousin and the situations that would come from it, he looked back, then at Anthony, lowered his face and answered, "No."

"And why is that Daniel?"

"Because fags aren't funny." Still looking down, Daniel turned around and walked away from his friend. Although it never felt well when such things happened, Anthony expected nothing less from the situation, as it always depended on the day and the crowd. This night, like many others, had worked itself to be one of those where he was the target, and everyone else seemed loaded with stones.

Walking back to the tables, Anthony saw his father sitting next to his mother and the adults were laughing and drinking. Getting close, he tapped his mother's shoulder and reported his current status.

"Mom, just so you know, and I'm not making it up, the other kids already made fun of me, and not even Daniel wants to play with me."

"Oh, honey."

"Come on, not again." Mehl overheard and put his two cents in. In fact, he doubled them. "Listen, you can't keep doing this every time we are out with other people." Mehl looked deeply into his son's eyes. "You need to deal with it. You need to be friends with the other kids and that's that."

"But Mom, they are always making fun of me. They made fun of my clothes."

"I told you. You and those stupid outfits you put on him."

"Mehl, be quiet." Julia looked into his husband's eyes and removed his hand from around her shoulder. "Baby," now talking to her son, "I'm sorry but you need to find somebody to play with. If it's not Daniel, then play with somebody new. Make friends, okay?"

"Yes ma'am." Anthony walked away from the table and sat on an elevated part of the concrete. Each event is similar as parents shove kids together and don't understand that kids are friends with other kids just because they are kids. That thought was never analyzed correctly, and in most cases, Anthony was the kid that nobody wanted to be around of. Like they said, Anthony was a fag, and fags aren't funny to be around of.

After a while, the barbecue was done and everyone was calling their kids to eat. Julia had garnered a nice plate for her son, and not playing with the other kids, Anthony was sitting and ready rather quickly. Sitting in front of his plate, he looked at the dark meat and the rice and potatoes and with large bites, devoured chunks at a time. This was the very instant when the noise of the surroundings and the city could be heard. Most of the kids were quiet and stuffing themselves and so were the adults. Anthony was tickled at the fact that everyone forgot about glamour when they ate. Not even if they tried to look good while doing it, as he saw around the tables, most people make the most absurd faces and ruffling breathing noises as well.

"Baby, how's the meat?"

"It's good mom."

"You like it?"

"Yes, tasty."

"Do you want me to cut them up into smaller pieces?"

"Aum, well—"

"Goddamn it, Julia. You do that way too much. Let the kid be and stop babying him."

"Here you go honey." The conversation ended at that, and Julia cut her son's meat anyway. Mehl appeared to be frustrated but kept on talking to the others, ignoring the two individuals to his right, Julia and Anthony.

Once the food was over with, the kids started running again and the adults chatting loudly. Julia stood up and removed the plate from underneath Anthony and told him to run along again. This time he did. Anthony was in rare form and he was angry and decided to tackle the entire crowd of kid's again. Walking closer he stood in the circle of kids and decided to blend in without worry. That wasn't the case.

"What are you doing here loser?" Jean exclaimed.

"I want to play."

"Well, we play hard, can you handle it?"

"Yes, I don't mind." There was silence and then Daniel spoke from under his cousin's watch.

"I don't think you should play. You will slow us down anyway."

"You guys are playing tag." Anthony smirked.

"Well, I just don't think you should."

Anthony took the hint, but walking away he felt the battle had just begun.

The night kept going strong and everything was the same, except for some people had left, including a chunk of the kids. The leftover ones were still running around the lot, but somehow seemed like a weaker front. Anthony didn't feel like trying again, but instead worked up his anger. He began walking around playing by himself and jumping, as he wasn't stepping on any crack or separation of the pavement. That kept him entertained and each time he began getting closer to the other kids, as they were running into the area in which he was playing. At one point Anthony saw Daniel standing looking away and jumped across a crack falling on his friend's back. As Daniel fell to the ground, Anthony apologized and kept playing.

"Sorry? What the hell was that?" Daniel questioned.

"Well, I'm playing and you got in the way, sorry."

"Well, I guess I'm sorry too," Daniel got closer and pushed Anthony on the ground. Some of the adults saw what happened and yelled from afar for them to stop. The kids laughed and went about their business.

"Really, really sorry." Daniel laughed. Anthony sat on the ground and he noticed his father looking at him with the same disappointment as usual. Anthony wasn't strong, he wasn't sporty, he couldn't play soccer like his father wanted and as currently obvious, wasn't popular nor liked around the kids. That stare torn his insides but fueled the anger he had worked up throughout the entire night. In one swift motion, he stood and without thinking it twice called out one name.

"Daniel!" The other boy turned and Anthony, in front of his face said "I'm not sorry for this," And punched him on the side of the face. Unprepared, Daniel walked back and his vibrant, blue eyes fought back. He punched Anthony in the stomach but the boy wasn't feeling a thing. Anthony grabbed Daniel by the arms and threw him on the ground. Daniel kicked and swirled but Anthony wasn't having any of it. While on the floor, he sat on Daniel's stomach and pinned his arms down. Daniel loosened them up and tried to move him from above, but still nothing happened. Finally, livid and drenched in his own wrath, Anthony grabbed Daniel by the hair and slammed his head on the ground. Time after time after time, he did this and heard his friend shriek in discomfort and pain. After what felt a while of this, Daniel freed himself from the grasp, and crawled out of it, only to move face down and having Anthony do it all again, repeatedly, banging his face on the ground.

"Stop that!" Marco pulled Anthony off his son and all of the kids were in awe of what had just happened. Julia also got close and grabbed her son to the side. After a couple of seconds had passed Marco took his son away and Julia, perplexed, softly questioned her son. "Anthony, please tell me what that was about."

"I-,'m…, I'm, just, just—"

"You can't do that. You understand me? You can't do that again, you hear me?"

"So, just-just, angr—"

"Tony, I know it's hard sometimes, but you can't fight your problems away. You need to face them like an adult. You need to be mature enough to let these feelings rinse off. You do not fix anything doing this. You understand?"

Anthony was still heaving from the strained conflict. His mother sat him on a chair next to her and he said nothing else. The party kept winding down and all he could hear were the comments the other women were making to his mother. "He was like a little animal." For a moment he felt content of what he did until he heard Marco screaming and Daniel inside one of the apartments.

"What the hell was that? You can't let people walk all over you this way. You can't be scared and let people beat you up. I've taught you better than that." Without a glitch he heard the man whip his son with his belt. "You will learn to be a man."

Driving home was quiet but he couldn't stop hearing everything that had happened inside of his head. The kids teasing him, his father reprimanding him, the kids rooting for the fight, the adults telling him to stop, his friend's shrieks when he slammed his head onto the ground; everything seemed to resonate with a hint of guilt. Throughout all of that, he knew the worst was hearing Daniel get hurt by his own father after their own fight. Not only because he had instigated the fight, but because he was aware that although he had similar father issues, he never had to worry about getting beat by his own father.

Mehl had said nothing else for the rest of the night, but as Anthony caught a glimpse of his face through the review mirror, he didn't need to as his smile said it all. Anthony looked out the window at the stars and couldn't help but smile at what he had learned tonight, his father did join him somehow.

Mr. Chess Kills My Insides

White. I opened my eyes and all I could see was white. The ceiling in its splendor staring back at me. Before I had a chance to rub my eyes to remove the webs off, a third arm stretched out across my belly. Still half asleep, I raised my head up slightly trying to figure out where it came from then, BAM! A third hand slammed into my nose. *Holy Shh-.* How could I have forgotten; I sat up on my bed holding onto my twisted nose and looking to either side I saw my twin cousins battling in their sleep. The boys were hyperactive even when unconscious. It was a funny sight since they looked nothing like one another. Always, I thought about having a twin of my own and looking directly at it by looking at my own skin, at my own imperfections. Rolling my eyes I cautiously opened the cocoon created around my face. I tried it out, and yes, victory, I could still breathe through my nose. I could still smell from it! *Wait, what is that yummy smell?* Still in my bedroom, I paced around aimlessly as I tried to wake up before attempting to go down the stairs and rolling down a step at a time. *Wash my face? Brush my teeth? What's the point if I'm eating breakfast soon? I'll brush them then.* I thought after maneuvering my exit from my crowded bed that I was going to be readily awake. I had to bend, stretch and elongate my limbs like the most astute spider trying to let the boys sleep longer. A moment of silence would be great. Though I achieved an early sense of awareness, my eyes were still slanted and glued from the corners up until the middle of them. My head still felt fuzzy, most likely because of the feeling of skin sleeping as I was awake. I rubbed it furiously but I was still thinking about nothing.

Opening the curtains slowly, I looked out the front of our house and saw the sunlight beaming its gray tint toward my face. The clouds were apparent but the temperature still hot. Through the glass strips that made up our house windows I saw the early birds out and about. *What time is it?* The old lady from across the street, she held her shopping bags and walked two centimeters per ten seconds of time. What a life. I tried to examine the context of her bags, hoping to see the ingredients to the ice pops she sold to all the kids in the neighborhood. I remembered my late grandmother taking me there whenever we visited her, in the house we now lived in. As I would rave about them, she would hold my arm reprimanding me and saying "It's just ice and flavoring. Most likely Cool-Aid, you could make it yourself." Without even looking at her I would always tell her that there had to be a secret ingredient. They were just too good! Then she would say with a stern tone "Well, that works for me, I'm not making them for you." To my disappointment, I was not a an owl, and I couldn't catch anything from my window.

I sat on my rocking chair and began to kneel, holding my legs together and resting my head upon my knees. The house was very silent then. Still sitting, I looked at the television's black screen. I would usually turn it on in the morning, but not today. The silence felt nice. It was Sunday and I was enjoying the moment. The television could wait. Instead, I slowly got up from the chair and walked over to my toy shelves, and through the glass inspected that all of the series were in their designed spaces. All of the figures were looking like I liked them to. I then smiled looking at the twins sleeping, and walking toward my sock drawer. I opened it and by removing just a pair of them I could see the key to the lock to the toy shelves. What a kid, I was more worried about preserving everything that was given to me and cared more about them than a parent. I was an old boy, I knew that. Suddenly, I turned as the wind howled and the curtains slowly opened as they lifted upon the rocking chair, then slowly began scratching the open space to stay up and flying high. By then the warm wind caressed me and with it came a smell. *Breakfast!*

Exiting the room, I grabbed the edge of the door and left it ajar. Now in the main corridor of the second floor, where the rooms were, I looked as if to hear with my eyes and nothing came toward me. No sounds, no shadows, no presence. Up to my right hand side was my parents bedroom. I crept my head in and with my entire body still outside the room I called out "Mom?" but nothing came. *This house is big, but where is everybody?*

Then, I walked across their bedroom door toward my sister's. Nothing. The guest bedroom. Nothing. The bathroom. *Oh, I have to pee!*

With the toilet still flushing I began to make my way down the stairs. The marble floors tingled my every nerve. Walking meant barefoot, and though the temperature is always the same, hot, the steps were always liberating from those facts known. With each step I could feel my eyes open wider. The window looking down the stairs let the light reflect in a way that made the white look like snow and the rest shine, blinding the world around it. It took me probably four minutes to walk down a set of twenty steps. It's safe to say I was enjoying the cool breeze sweeping through my insides each and every second I was standing upon these steps made of clouds. The sky at my very own feet.

Once downstairs, I began to hear whispers. Then *HAHAHAHA*. Well, safe to say mother was awake. *AHHH HAHAHAHA*. As was my aunt. *AHHHHH!!* And my other aunt. The chatter increased as I got closer to the kitchen. The place where families grow fonder of each other. The noise level was so high I questioned my hearing earlier. I guess I was really seeping in the quiet upstairs.

"Good morning honey!!" my mom was always as tender in the morning as she was at night. "Did you sleep okay?"said she kissing my cheek. I heard her only, avoiding the rest of the voices making God knows what comments. Most likely to the effect of sleeping too much or other ridiculous morning words that only upset a half sleep, very hungry child. I smiled and stopped myself from asking where the rest of the family was. Better me find them than starting a conversation I would never get out of. I asked for my blessings from my aunts, kissed and hugged them and walked through the kitchen toward the back room. This area held the laundry room, a spare room, a spare bathroom and a sitting area that was only used to put groceries on when we brought them in from the car. I walked into the outside area, walking by all the parked cars and following the deeper voices and lower laughter. Getting closer I couldn't hear that of my father. I peered through the corner and saw my uncles talking about the weather, the grass, seeds and then moving on to carburetors and engines. Before it was too late, I walked my way back into the house.

Through a window I looked at the outside patio and saw our two bitches sunbathing, and the other dog, the male, making holes through the dirt. His snout suddenly looked up and blackened, enjoyed the current, quick-lived breeze. Then without any movement, his entire body started trembling and with one fire shot his nose exploded. Disgusted at the sight I whispered to myself *Bless you* and walked toward the dinning room. Opening another door, I looked into the living room, on the floor there were three bodies shaped like a sunflower. The girls looked up at me and my sister along with my cousins said hi in unison and carried on with their business.

I began to worry. I had seen my father's car parked when I went outside. *Did I miss some place?* As I walked thinking, my aunt abruptly crossed paths with me at the bottom of the steps and told me with a smile "I bet those boys are still dead asleep. It is now after one in the afternoon and they need to be out and about." With that she patted my head and went upward. I stood there thinking about the noise becoming more and more apparent. I needed to get away. I wasn't done with my Sunday morning. No matter what time it was. Then, I heard a loud throat clearing sound. *Dad!* I moved slightly to my left and put my ear upon the wooden door. The sound came rougher this time. I knocked on the door and waited three seconds for a response. Nothing. Another knock and my father's voice quivered loudly "Come in!" I turned the knob thinking how stupid I had been, of course he was in his study.

After closing the door behind me and siting I saw my father remove his glasses, putting them on the table and moving slightly toward my direction in his brown, leather, master chair. The chair was huge and intimidating. As was walking into my father's study when obviously he didn't want to be bothered. I sat on the chair facing him across the desk and looked into his blue eyes.

"Bendicion papa, buenos dias."

"Dios te bendiga." His voice wasn't the same. I noticed within his words that his diction had changed. Also, when he opened his small mouth to speak I noticed his tongue was three times its normal size.

"Are you okay? What's wrong with your tongue?"

"I think I have some kind of an allergic reaction. I also have a fever and a pounding headache, so don't try me today."

Out of all days, he was sick when there were two sets of extra family, including six additional children. I sympathized to his feelings. I stood up and reaching out my hand across the desk met his own resting upon it.

"Do you want something to drink?"

He smirked and pointed with his eyes toward a coffee mug on the side.

"Are you taking something?"

His smile now apparent moved up and down with his head. I stood silently and then removing my hand from upon his went back to sit down. The room was quiet for a little until laughter arose and the rambunctious twins ran down the stairs which stood behind me in the study. I rolled my eyes the way only I could and then looked around the room hoping they wouldn't find me there. I looked around the room with incentive, avoidance. The door, the book shelves that began to the right of it and ended behind the desk, the desk, my father, his eyes. My father's gaze was coldly. He was not an easy guy. I knew he liked me being there, but he was questioning whether I was liking it. Our relationship was never that great. So I sat looking at him, enjoying the moment, but questioning whether he was.

"Okay, I know I rather not talk and since you are here, we could do something, right? Come on let me show you something. Come on, drag that chair closer."

My father's chair twirled toward the left and without ever getting up he removed an old wooden box upon a shelf and twirling back, placed it upon the desk. He opened the box and some particularly familiar guys could be seen from inside. He looked at me and smiled with his eyes.

"Do you want me to teach you how to play Chess?"

I nodded upward excitedly. Knowing he was teaching me something that did not involve a plastic ball was good news to me.

"Whoa, were those *nono*'s?"

"Yes, this belonged to your grandfather. And if you like them, one day you will own them too."

"Really?"

"Yes, I'm not lying." My father coughed and I realized I shouldn't make him talk very much.

"Well, I'm sure I'm really going to like it."

He took all the pieces out of the wooden box and placed the board upon the desk. All of it was wood. The pieces were all perfectly carved. I took one and without knowing what it did I held it dearly knowing the quality of these pieces. Whether it was the work done on it or my grandfather's invisible fingerprints, it was mesmerizing to me.

My father asked for the piece and once I gave it to him he finished the now adorned chess board. It looked beautiful though very intimidating.

"Okay, are you ready?"

"Yes!"

"Well, I'm going to go first and then you will. Don't worry I'll let you know how to move the pieces."

"Okay."

He grabbed his glasses from the desk and put them on his face. My father moved one of his little guys and then directed me with his head to do a similar move. After three of his pawns and three of mine were making their way, he moved one ahead of the rest.

"Dad, why did you do that? Don't you need to move the other ones you haven't touched? Don't you have to move them one at a time? Why would you do that? Why?"

"Those pieces can do that."

"So I can move from here to here?" with that I took my first moved pawn and slid it three places ahead.

"No!" My father shouted with aggravation. "You can't do that. Only one space at a time."

I apologized and moved my pawn two spaces back. He then moved his horse ahead of a pawn.

"No. You can't do that dad. The pawn is in front of the horse and you can't move it until the pawn is moved too."

"The horse, is actually a knight, and I moved it in the shape of an L because that is what they do" said he amid sighs.

"Oh. Cool."

"Okay, wait, let's start over."

My father replaced the pieces to their designated staring positions. He had realized that he had taken too many steps ahead without giving me the basics of the game. He was a brilliant man. A brilliant man but an awful teacher. He could teach you to do something as he had the knowledge, but his patience was uncanny and his temper took the best of him.

"Okay, starting over" said he removing six pieces from the board. All the same colors.

"This one is a pawn. They sort of hold the front to the more important people. They are like soldiers."

"Like the green ones I have!"

"Yes son, like toy soldiers. Now, they can move one space at a time. Though, if it is the first move for them, you can move them two spaces ahead."

"Oh, well, so the soldiers do have more options to begin with, they just have to use it quickly or their chance is gone. Okay. I get it."

He carried on about how they diagonally take other pieces. Yes, he keep reassuring me, the point of the game was to take all the pieces or work your way to get the king. He then showed me the basics to a en-passant and how the rules might change a little bit. But he was stern reminding me "you have to do it right after the move. If you wait on your next move, you can't." Lastly, he mentioned the pawns could be upgraded if they made it to the opposing side. He quickly gave up after I asked a hundred questions about variations and stubborn attempts to find a loop to prove his theory wrong. When he stopped, he coughed louder than the first time and I realized I was losing my goal. Don't make him talk too much.

"Okay, so this is the rook."

"Can I call it the tower?"

"Yes, you may. Now, there are only two at each corner and they move forward or sideways, in a straight line."

"That's cool."

"Yes, very nifty indeed."

"I think I like those the most."

"Wait, you'll need to judge all of them before you pick a favorite."

"Okay."

"These are the knights."

"Oh come on! What's with the names? I will call those horses."

"Yes, quite obvious, eh? Yes, they are very tricky. Like I showed you briefly before they can move in the shape of an L like so."

After showing me on the board I questioned the L saying "So you have to land on the tip of the L not one spot ahead of it?"

"Correct. Good, you are getting the moves. You'll be playing in no time. Now, these are the bishops. They move in diagonal lines, like this" he showed me on the board. "But remember, they can't jump other pieces."

"Those are boring. Why would they be so close to the royal people pieces? Those moves are lame."

"Now, the queen. She, is the most powerful piece. She can move in any straight line, like the bishop and the rook. Or like you call them, the tower and the "boring ones" he let out a laugh that caused him to cough up louder for longer this time. I stood up not liking to see him sick. He was such a strong man. So tall, so thick, so strong. Seeing him vulnerable, which he rarely let happen, made me feel just like earlier, when I couldn't find him. Lost. Alone. Fearing the world.

"Okay, okay, I'm fine" he dismissed the coughs with a throat sound and kept going "so, she can move in any straight line."

"Yes, you were right, she seems pretty prepared to defeat the enemy's forces!" and with the stroke of a hand an invisible sword appeared as to make my point.

"Focus. Lastly, is the king. The one everyone needs to get. You are after him because that marks the end of the game."

"And what does *he* do?"

"Well, just like any strong force in the world, he has his weaknesses. He is chained to only one move. He is stuck with moving like the queen, in a straight line, but, he can only do one space at a time."

"Well, that's limiting."

"Okay, enough chatter, let's play."

The first round was still very much aggravating to my father. I questioned everything and had forgotten half of the moves already. He had impulses of grabbing the board and slamming it against the wall with rage. Instead, he coughed louder and louder. The second game was on its way and two of my pawns and one of my horses, my knight, were taken.

I looked at the lonely pawn I had taken away from him. Suddenly, the twin's voices could be heard getting closer. They loudly questioned my whereabout and called out my name. They got closer to the study's door and hesitated to knock on it. My father heard it and tried his best to ignore it. I knew that if they had gone in my father's fumes would have burned us all alive. They kept talking to each other "you open it!", "No, you do it!" Father's face was now directed toward the door and then my mother's voice was heard outside.

"Hey! Do not go in there. Uncle is very sick and needs his space. Now go on, find your cousin elsewhere!"

She knocked on the door a moment after and came in. She looked at my father with a smile as if asking how he felt or maybe sympathizing with him. She cocked her head to the right and though surprised she did not jump, but smile.

"Oh. You are here. Well, what are you guys doing?"she said this while she looked at the desk. "Great! You are having a moment. Well, good, you need more of those." While looking at my father with her words she walked toward me and kissed me on the forehead. She then proceeded to walk toward father's side and grabbed his head placing it upon her bosom. He obliged and before a child's comfort was written on his face he opened his eyes and patted her back as if to tell her *that's enough*.

She got the hint and hugged him slightly. She began to make her way out of the room while still looking at the board and said "Good bishop move son. You know, those are my favorites!"

Once she was out of the room my father's shoulders took the same shape as from before any noise or anybody knew we were in there. He concentrated on his next move and I asked him.

"Which one is your favorite piece?" Before he had a chance to answer I spoke again.

"Well, I'll tell you mine. I thought about it. I think I would prefer to be the queen. She has the most freedom, everybody fears her and she is the main force protecting the king!"

My father sat back and removed his glasses once more. Sitting back in his chair, I could tell something was coming. He was very selective with words. Very few. Me, on the other hand, talked plenty, yet I retained his selectiveness. It was just abundant selectiveness. He cocked his head and with his right hand providing them, he began to bite the end of his glass. The next second his left hand began to massage his throat. He didn't say a word.

Silence being the main course in the room was not rare, so I sat waiting. My legs began to tremble, moving up and down rapidly. My tick took over my arms as I started to put my hands together and with my fingers touching each tip.

The leather screeched and I stopped my twitching.

"You know, though you are right, the queen is not that important. Yes, her appearance is very intimidating *but* she is nothing once she's gone. The game itself is based on taking the king out. If so is fulfilled, the queen and her gracious moves mean nothing. *He* is limited, but you have to remember that a man, a king, a god, most likely has an Achilles' heel. Meaning, that they have a downfall, a disability. And although he is high and mighty, he can only move selectively. With that said, I think it's more important to remember that your limiting existence is not as bad as you may think. And if fearing it means that you forget the greatness brought from knowing once you are gone, everyone is doomed, then you need to think about that. It is better to die with purpose and live with limitation than live with everything and die for nothing. No gift."

I understood his direction but not his words. Before I had a chance to question him I saw him putting everything away.

"But we are not done playing!" I protested.

"I think we are. Go on, play with your cousins. They won't be here for much longer. They all leave tomorrow. Go enjoy the summer days and let me get back to work here."

I understood, he had given his lesson and now he needed to be alone. I smiled and helped him put the pieces away. He packed it all and placed it upon his desk in an organized manner. I walked toward him and thanked him. With a kiss on the cheek, I hugged him tightly knowing we had a moment in time I would take me with always. He kissed and hugged me back. His tongue was still enlarged and for some reason by being closer to him I could taste differently. Like rusty metal. I felt bad for him and walked toward the door.

I turned the knob and he whistled at me. I turned around and with high strung eyebrows exclaimed "Yes?"

"Here." He took the board and the wooden box and extended it toward me. "I think you can practice for our next match."

I took the gift with pride and without a word looked at him, smiled and walked out of the room. The wooden door closed. There never was a another game.

The grass is rusty, brown like rotten metal. I walk on it slowly, and it's crisp. The sky blinds me with tremendous strength. The clouds seem filled with light instead of water. They are still gray, just neon sign clouds. The clouds race through the sky as if racing toward the end of time. The wind with them burns my face. It's pretty cold today. The November rain turns to puffs every now and then. I like it. I always have. Before and always, the season gets me.

The walkway I've created with each step on the grass disappears behind me. I'll have to do it all over again. There are patches of grass holding onto their green. They will try to defy the season, the reasons, and expectancy. I would do that if I were grass. I do that now as I am a man.

Today is just another day. The years keep passing by and I can't remember anything. People say this feeling comes when you're older, fearing the end that's coming near. Mid-life crisis, I've heard them say. But I'm still young by standards and yet still feel the same. My years left with the neon clouds, with the freezing air and the warmer wind that I get less of each year. Unlike before.

The grass is dead here. There is absolutely nothing alive in here. Above it or below it. The ground is sustained by the physics of erosion. My emotions still vividly attentive. The grass here is dead. Just like the rest within it.

It's been roughly thirteen years. Such a questioning boy. Now, a persistent man. Time does scrape our bodies and with that our minds shrink slightly, trying to sponge out the thoughts, memories, hopes and dreams created in past or current lives. It's a fearful existence. And those memories are too important to lose. Time does wither down the bees, the flowers, the pollen, the honey. It steals the greenest of apples and tallest of trees. Time is the trickiest tool and the oldest way of being.

It's been roughly too long to forget and too early to remember all the signs hanging in front of me and the symbols calling out my name. *Come here* they say. *Come see this.* The experimentation has left me wondering.

Regardless of the digits attached to my name, I've perfected my theories quite well. But there is one that keeps me prisoner. Death.

The grass is dead here. There is absolutely nothing alive in here. Above it or below it. My destination is quite clear. I place the flowers upon the dirt and sit down upon the ground that has become *you.*

The tombstone reads a name. A creator. A philosopher. A teacher. A brilliant man. A stubborn man. An angry man. A loving man. *Father, I miss you.*

It's been roughly thirteen years since you taught me the reason for your existence. With pieces of wood, the one to rotten was you. The grass is completely dead.

A sudden demise. Going away with so much meaning. A dramatic end dooming the world.

I remember in one year, the struggles that you faced. The protection the other ones could provide. A daughter as a knight. Free like a wild horse. A lover like a bishop, so strong and poised. Breaking the rules to find a way. You've had your pawns. You'd be surprised to know, you changed lives.

The dirt feels wet, the wind still floats in front of me. I'm ready again. With my right, index finger I scrape the blackened snow. I'm holding on to your knowledge.

I'm ready to play, the queen that without you is simply useless.

LaVergne, TN USA
11 April 2011
223656LV00002B/203/P

9 781607 493211